VIOLET INVESTIGATES

.·. The Pearl of The Orient .·.

THIS BOOK BELONGS TO

....

HARRIET WHITEHORN
ILLUSTRATED BY BECKA MOOR

SIMON AND SCHUSTER

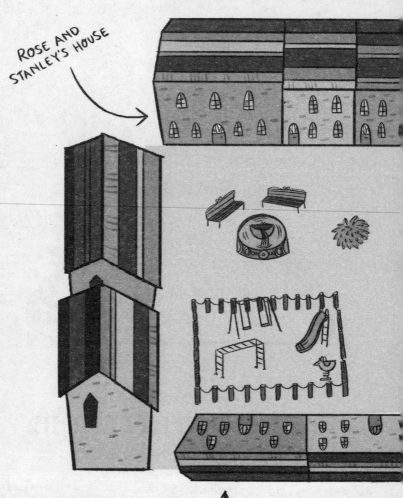

ROSE AND STANLEY'S HOUSE

CHARLOTTE'S FLAT

DU PLICITOUS HOUSE

DEE DEE'S FLAT

LYDIA AND BEATRICE'S HOUSE

STELLA AND BEN'S HOUSE

VIOLET'S HOUSE

FOR CLARA – HW

FOR MUM – BM

First published in Great Britain in
2014 by Simon & Schuster UK Ltd
This edition published in 2022

1 3 5 7 9 10 8 6 4 2

Simon & Schuster UK Ltd
1st Floor, 222 Gray's Inn Road
London
WC1X 8HB

www.simonandschuster.co.uk
www.simonandschuster.com.au
www.simonandschuster.co.in

Simon & Schuster Australia, Sydney
Simon & Schuster India, New Delhi

A CIP catalogue record for this book is available from the British Library.

PB ISBN 978-1-3985-1846-9
eBook ISBN 978-1-4711-1896-8
eAudio ISBN 978-1-4711-7645-6

Printed and bound by CPI Group (UK) Ltd, Croydon, CRO 4YY

MIX
Paper from
responsible sources
FSC
FSC® C171272

This is a story about Violet Remy-Robinson.

Violet lives with a cat named Pudding (short for Sticky Toffee Pudding), her mother, Camille Remy, who is a jewellery designer, and her father, Benedict Robinson, who is an architect.

They live in a very stylish and incredibly tidy flat and there is a large garden at the back of Violet's flat that she shares with all the other children and grown-ups who live around it.

Violet's best friend is Rose, whose family live in the same street and who goes to the same school as Violet.

MON	TUES	WEDS	THURS
Archery + climbing	Russian dancing + chess	Tai chi + mandarin	Flamenco dancing + violin

Violet does a great many activities after school. In fact, she's so busy that she has a special calendar in her room to make sure she knows where she has to be every day.

Climbing is Violet's favourite thing to do which is why she goes twice a week. Violet is an only child, and so spends a lot of time with grown-ups. This is sometimes a bit boring, but it also means that she's learnt some very useful things, such as how to read a menu in French, mix a perfect cocktail

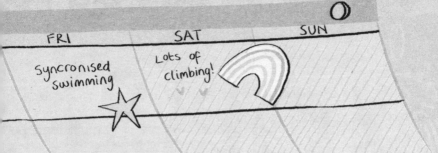

FRI

Syncronised swimming

SAT

Lots of climbing!

SUN

and play poker. While her parents are at work, Violet is looked after by Norma the housekeeper, who does not say much, but when she does say something it is well worth listening to.

Norma also makes the most delicious food. A wise person once told Violet that you can tell a lot about a person by their favourite food, so to introduce you properly to all the people in this story, I thought I would tell you about their very favourite things to eat.

VIOLET

CAMILLE

Big juicy steak with extremely thin chips. And sticky toffee pudding (which may give you a clue as to how Pudding got his name...).

Plain cheese and tomato pizza, hot crumpets with melted butter, ice cream sundaes, roast chicken.

BENEDICT

GODFATHER JOHNNY

Sushi (very neatly arranged).

ROSE

Mini rolls, salt and vinegar crisps and spaghetti Bolognese.

Coffee walnut cake and whisky, preferably together. Roast chicken.

GODMOTHER CELESTE

Her mother's Poulet au Vinaigre (which she misses very much).

THE COUNT DU PLICITOUS

CHICKEN LIVERS, CAVIAR AND SNAILS (YUCK).

THE COUNTESS DU PLICITOUS

DOESN'T OFTEN EAT FOOD, PREFERS PROTEIN SHAKES, WHICH TASTE LIKE PECULIAR MILKSHAKES.

ISABELLA DU PLICITOUS

PC GREEN

KEEPS IT SIMPLE WITH FISH FINGERS, OVEN CHIPS AND BAKED BEANS.

FANCY FOOD SUCH AS LOBSTER SPAGHETTI AND CAVIAR WITH TRUFFLE OIL.

NORMA THE HOUSEKEEPER

LOVES FRIED CHICKEN AND SPICY NOODLE SOUP.

DEE DEE DEROTA

BANANA SANDWICHES, CHEESY WOTSITS AND CHERRY BAKEWELLS. BUT HER FAVOURITE TREAT IS BATTENBERG CAKE.

But come, enough talk about food (which is making me very hungry indeed), let us get on with the story . . .

It all Begins with a Fox at a Window.

First, you must picture a tall oak tree in a beautiful garden.

It is late spring when the story begins so the tree should be covered in fluttery green leaves. And now you must imagine a girl of around ten, small for her age and slim, with dark brown hair, straight as a ruler, olive skin and precise brown eyes. And then turn that girl upside down, set her swinging to and fro from a high branch of the tree, holding on

7

only by her knees, shamelessly showing off to a crowd of children gathered at the bottom. And there you have Violet Remy-Robinson at the start of the story.

The names of the children watching were Lydia, Charlotte, Ben, Stanley and Stella, and they were known as the 'midders'. The children who lived in the houses around the garden were all different ages; the midders were seven to eleven years old, and anyone younger than them was a 'littilee' and anyone older was a 'twelver'. But at that moment it was only the midders who were watching Violet, because the littlies had been gathered up for tea and baths and the twelvers were loafing around by the swings, showing off to each other and chatting about whatever twelvers chat about.

Anyway, back to Violet, whose tree-climbing antics were being watched with open mouths, and a tense mixture of fear and excitement. Six months before, when she had climbed up that particular tree (showing off as she was now) Violet had fallen. Fallen badly. And then there had been the fantastic excitement of blood, broken bones and an ambulance.

The person I haven't mentioned, because she was sitting apart from the others, is Rose Trelawney, Violet's best friend. Rose was slight like Violet, but had long hair and large, nervous blue eyes. Unlike the others, Rose was definitely not watching Violet, no thank you! It was far too anxious-making and scary, and Rose was as timid as Violet was bold. So instead of watching, Rose was playing with her cat, The Major, and Violet's cat, Pudding. As she tickled their tummies,

she wished silently that Violet would hurry up and get safely down from the tree before a grown-up caught her and there was a huge telling-off. Because Rose hated being told off.

So why had Violet ignored the strict warnings by her parents and numerous doctors forbidding her to climb trees? Well, the answer was that her arch enemy, Stanley – who also happened to be Rose's older brother – had dared her, taunting her that girls were too stupid and cowardly to climb trees. And impulsive Violet, her cheeks flaming red with fury at his insults, couldn't just walk away like a sensible person might. Oh no, she had to prove him wrong.

SO ANNOYING!

The dare had been to reach the top of the tree and Violet was still a little way off, so she finished swinging, put herself back the right way round and steadied her head against the trunk's cool bark until the world stopped spinning.

'Come on, get a move on! Or are you too scared?' Stanley mocked from the ground.

Violet didn't bother to reply; she was far too busy concentrating on not falling. And her previously broken arm was aching terribly from all the effort. The top of the tree was near and the branches were becoming twiggy. She stepped onto one that gave way with an almighty . . .

CRACK!

Violet lurched forward, grabbing wildly at branches. Her audience let out enormous gasps as they watched her only just save herself by a whisker. Rose winced. Tom, one of the older boys, appeared at the bottom of the tree and called up to check Violet was okay. Stanley, meanwhile, looked delighted.

'I'm fine, Tom,' Violet called back with more confidence that she felt. She glared at Stanley. 'Don't panic, nearly there, you can do it,' she told herself strictly, while gingerly testing another branch with her foot. It was reassuringly solid so she hauled herself up, right to the top of the tree, and poked her head out of the leafy ceiling to survey the view. The garden

spread out beneath her like a grassy picnic blanket. She gazed around, delighting as ever in the feeling of being at the top of something very tall.

Then two things happened at the same time. The alarm bleeped on her watch, telling her that it was six-fifteen and she needed to go home or she would be late (again), and someone called her name. It was a man's voice, stern and with a foreign accent.

'Violet!' the voice reprimanded. She looked around to see Marek, one of the builders who worked with her father, leaning out of the window of the top floor of the Thomsons' old house. 'You know you are not supposed to be climbing that tree! Get down before I tell your father!' he shouted, but with a wink, so that Violet knew he was not really cross.

Violet smiled at him and was about to hurry back down the tree, when her attention was caught by a man standing next to Marek. He was middle-aged, with a pointed face, slicked-back wavy red hair and an intense gaze that was fixed upon her. Violet was struck by how much he looked like a fox.

The alarm on her watch bleeped again. She really had to go home otherwise she would be in big trouble. She lowered herself onto the

branch and carefully picked her way down the tree, trying not to rush. Everyone clapped and high-fived her as she jumped nimbly down to the grass. Rose breathed a large sigh of relief.

'Violet showed you, Stanley, didn't she?' Tom laughed.

Stanley was furious that he had been made to look foolish by a girl. 'You had better run, *Vileness*, or you'll be late for Mummy and Daddy,' he mocked.

Stanley was right, Violet thought as she ran off with a wave and a quick 'see you at school' to Rose. She did her last, very necessary piece of climbing for the evening; up the drainpipe on the back of her house, and through the open window into the bathroom, where Norma was waiting with Violet's bath already run.

'Very, very late,' Norma said, with a disapproving shake of her head.

'I know - I'm really really sorry,' Violet apologised, before plunging into the warm water.

Half-past six was a magical hour in the Remy-Robinson household.

As Camille, Violet's elegant and clever mama, was stepping daintily out of a taxi, heels clacking delicately on the pavement, Benedict, Violet's learned and successful papa, was softly closing his study door. They were both making their way to their immaculate white sitting room, where Norma would serve them a delicious cocktail and they would discuss their day with their darling daughter,

Violet, before eating a scrumptious supper.

The transformation that Norma had managed to make to Violet's appearance in just seven minutes was miraculous. When she stepped into the sitting room, Violet was perfectly clean and smelling of fig soap. Her hair had been combed to shiny smoothness and the old T-shirt, shorts and trainers that she had been wearing had been replaced with a sparkling white and purple dress and shiny lilac ballet pumps.

'Cherie!' Camille cried. 'A little late, but I can forgive you, as you look so beautiful.' She kissed Violet warmly on the cheek, enveloping her in a cloud of perfume. 'Come and meet our guests.'

Standing by the window, chatting to her father and with a cocktail in his hand, was the man who had been with Marek.

Oh no! Violet panicked. *He is going to tell my parents that he saw me up the tree and get me into loads of trouble!*

Violet was in such a dither that she hardly noticed a girl of around her own age and a tall, thin lady, standing next to the man. The lady was dressed in a tight leopard skin dress with a good deal of shiny gold jewellery, and her blonde hair was piled up on top of her head like a meringue. The girl had a pale, haughty face and long red hair, and wore a matching leopard skin dress.

Violet's father took his daughter's hand proudly. 'This is our daughter, Violet. Violet, this is Renard and Coraline, the Count and Countess Du Plicitous, and their daughter Isabella. They have bought the house just across the garden and have kindly asked me to re-design it for them.'

Isabella and her mother gave Violet quick, tight smiles that never quite reached their eyes. But the Count swept over to her and kissed her hand.

'*Enchanté*, my dear!' he said. Violet had to force herself not to snatch her hand away, for he had the most peculiar orangey-brown eyes she had ever seen, like an animal's.

He wore a pale purple jacket, with a crisp yellow rose in the buttonhole. He smiled broadly at Violet, showing his small, pointed teeth. The whole effect was really rather scary.

Violet smiled back as politely as she could, praying that the Count would not say anything about seeing her earlier in the garden.

To her relief, her father announced, 'Now, Count, shall we discuss some ideas? It's such a beautiful house, I am so excited.' He drew the Count aside for a lengthy discussion about room layouts and kitchen fittings.

The Countess began to chat to Camille.

'Renard tells me you are a jewellery designer for Smartier. I am so jealous! As you can see,' she said, jangling the bracelets on her wrist, 'I adore jewellery with a passion. I obviously don't need to work; Renard earns more than I could ever spend and besides, I'm far too busy looking after myself. But if I did work, I would do just what you do.'

'*Merci*, for the compliment,' Camille said with a smile. 'That is a magnificent ruby in your necklace. Really exquisite.'

'I know,' agreed the Countess smugly. 'Renard does spoil me and I do *so* love real jewellery. I could never wear anything fake. But I do happen to know of this amazing little man who is a genius at copying jewellery. He would be perfect for someone like you who probably can't afford the real thing. I think I have his card.' She started to rummage around in her pink snakeskin handbag.

Violet was impressed that her mother managed to keep a polite smile on her face, because she thought the Countess was being incredibly rude. *Poor Isabella*, she thought, *imagine having a mother like that!* So, trying to be nice, she turned to the girl.

'I'm so pleased you're moving in. It'll be great to have another girl in the garden. The boys are always ganging up on us. I'll have to introduce you to my best friend Rose and to—'

Isabella interrupted her. 'I go to boarding school actually and I stay there most weekends to do extra activities and play in matches – I'm captain of all the teams,' she boasted. 'And then in the holidays we either go skiing or stay on our yacht. Besides, I don't think my mother would want me playing with garden children.' She crinkled her nose as if she could smell something awful.

Oh no! thought Violet. *Isabella is worse than the Countess.* She was about to invent some very urgent homework that she had to go and finish, but Camille, who had been half-listening to their conversation, shot her a look that said, *I know they seem awful, but please make an effort*. So Violet took a deep breath and tried to think of something else to say.

Just at that moment Pudding jumped through the window. Isabella looked at him with distaste as he weaved around her legs. 'We have a Siamese cat called Chiang-Mai, he is exceptionally handsome and incredibly intelligent, with the finest pedigree that money can buy. What breed of cat is that?'

'Oh, he's not a pedigree. He's just a moggy. We found him abandoned in the garden when he was a kitten,' Violet replied.

'Hmmm, I'm not surprised he was left

there. He's a very ugly cat!'
Isabella laughed for the first
time. 'Mummy,' she said,
interrupting her mother's
conversation with Camille.
'Do look at their hideous
cat!'

The Countess looked at
Pudding and burst into a *hee-haw hee-haw* laugh, sounding
rather like a donkey.

Violet wanted to say
something very rude back,
but before she could think
of something suitable the

Countess turned to her. 'So, Violet, what are you good at? Do you play sport?' She looked at Violet quizzically. 'Clearly not netball; you are much too short!' And she laughed her donkey laugh again.

Violet had had enough. 'I am of course much too short to do any sport at all, so I spend all my time playing poker, Countess.' Then she watched with amusement as the Countess's face became a picture of horror, mixed with disbelief.

'Violet!' Camille reprimanded gently. 'She is only joking, Countess. Chess is Violet's game and you are very good at climbing too, aren't you? We joke that Violet is part monkey.'

'Oh, what a coincidence! Isabella is an excellent climber! In fact she has represented England at a junior level,' the Countess purred.

'How impressive,' Camille replied, elbowing Violet before her daughter could roll her eyes. 'Poor Violet broke her arm very badly a couple of months ago, falling out of the tree in the garden by your new house. She is forbidden to climb up trees by the doctors for two more weeks and by me, ever again. She's now only allowed to climb on the wall at the sports centre, where she can wear a harness.'

Overhearing, the Count raised an eyebrow at Violet, who blushed deeply. But Camille didn't notice.

'Violet is great friends with Dee Dee Derota, your new neighbour,' she said to the Countess.

'What, that weird old lady in the basement flat?' the Countess exclaimed, her face wrinkling up in disgust. 'How peculiar. She's a dreadfully selfish woman. She wouldn't let us have her flat and we are desperate to put a swimming pool down there. It's so important for Isabella to practise her diving.'

Violet flushed bright red again, this time with fury. How dare the Countess refer to Dee Dee as weird! Rather eccentric maybe, but not weird.

'I thought Isabella was never at home?' Violet snapped. 'She was telling me she's always on your yacht. Can't she practise her diving off that?'

The Countess waved Violet away as if she were an annoying fly. 'Although, I have to say that what's-her-name, Doo Doo, does have one of the most spectacular pieces of jewellery I have ever seen. But of course, you must know this already, Camille?'

Violet's mother looked surprised and shook her head. 'No, I didn't know.'

The Countess looked amazed, and continued conspiratorially. 'Well, you won't believe this, but she has one of the most valuable—'

'I thought Mrs Derota was a most charming lady,' the Count interrupted. 'Coraline, my darling, I think we have taken up enough of this enchanting family's time. Thank you so much for the cocktails, Camille, Benedict. Oh, and Violet?' He turned his strange orange eyes on her. 'Be sure to listen to your mother's advice. Don't go climbing any more trees.'

After supper, when Violet came back into the sitting room to say goodnight to her parents, she found a card lying on the floor. It was thick card with black swirly lettering.

Mr
Frederick Orger
Master
Costume Jeweller

Telephone:
1234 JEWEL

'What's this?' Violet asked, showing it to her mother.

'Oh, that's the card the Countess gave me. It's for the

man who specialises in costume jewellery.' Camille tucked the card behind the clock on the mantelpiece.

'Didn't you think the Du Plicitouses were horrible?' Violet asked.

Her mother was silent for a moment. 'Sometimes you have to meet people a few times to get to know them. Please be nice to Isabella. It's not easy being new, you must try and make her feel welcome.'

Violet sighed. She wasn't sure her mother was right at all, but she would do her best to get along with the Du Plicitous family.

3
A BUNCH OF YELLOW ROSES

Dee Dee Derota had been a starlet in Hollywood in the 1950s ('I was a beauty then, not that you'd know it now.'), married an American film director, Dave Derota ('I stole him off Marilyn Monroe, she was furious.'), and lived a happy and glamorous life until Dave sadly died at the ripe old age of eighty-five ('That's what you get if you marry a man twenty years older than you: a long widowhood.'). Dee Dee soon decided she had had enough of America and its endless sunshine, hamburgers and health food. She missed grey skies, drizzly rain and a decent cup of tea, so she returned home to London.

And that is how she came to live with her spoilt Persian cat, Lullabelle, in a messy basement flat, crammed full of strange furniture, old clothes, handbags, shoes, jewellery, books, records, magazines, make-up, beauty products and pretty much anything else you could think of. But despite the mess – or perhaps because of it – Violet adored going there, often with Rose. They liked to rummage around, trying on clothes and jewellery, drinking endless cups of sugary tea, eating Battenberg cake and cheesy wotsits.

And Dee Dee was always delighted to see them.

The day after the Count and Countess had visited her parents, in the very short gap of time between the end of her chess lesson and half-past six, Violet went to visit Dee Dee.

'Let yourself in darlin', I'm in here!' Dee Dee called, when Violet knocked on her door. She found the old lady lying on her purple velvet sofa, her red hair in curlers and her

face covered in a face mask that looked like strawberry jelly. Dee Dee proceeded to pull it off in wobbly strips, which Violet found rather revolting, so she focused instead on the enormous bunch of yellow roses that had appeared on a small table in Dee Dee's sitting room.

'Aren't they just ravishin'?' Dee Dee sighed in the Southern belle accent that she had cultivated during her Hollywood years.

'It was so darlin' of the Count to give them to me.'

'I hear you've met the Count and Countess?' Violet asked, examining a bottle of emerald-green nail varnish and stepping over Lullabelle, who was sprawled on the swirly pink carpet.

'Of course, darlin'. They are my new landlords. In fact, they tried to get me to leave my flat so that they could make a basement swimming pool or something ridiculous. The Count was quite rude and angry when I said no.' She paused, taking out her rollers. 'But now we are the best of friends, especially since he sent me those gorgeous roses. His wife is so glamorous, I felt quite the scruff and their daughter is obviously very talented.' Dee Dee unfailingly saw the best in people. She patted her perfect copper curls with an immaculately manicured hand. 'Now I need to put my face on, before anyone catches me looking so dreadful.' And she proceeded to apply a good deal of makeup including false eyelashes.

'Well I think they are the most awful people I have ever met,' Violet announced.

'Now, Violet, you must not be so rude about people.

And where are my manners? Please go and help yourself to a little something from the kitchen, and then have you got time to play dress-up? I found the most gorgeous blush-coloured evening dress, covered in gold sequins, that I thought would look exquisite on you. I wore it to see a boxing match in Vegas with Frank Sinatra.'

Violet was about to reply, when her watch alarm bleeped. 'Sorry, Dee Dee,' she said. 'I have to go home for supper. Norma will be so cross if I'm late again.' And with that she planted a quick kiss on the old lady's powdery cheek and ran out of the door.

4
THE PEARL OF THE ORIENT

Spring smoothed into summer and the temperature soared. A heavy heat descended and the cool greenness of the garden became tinged with yellowy-brown, despite the constant swish-swashing of sprinklers. Most of the grown-ups took on a damp, cross look and even the children preferred flopping about in the shade to charging around.

Life continued as usual for Violet in a whirlwind of school, tests and her after-school activities.

Meanwhile the Count and Countess Du Plicitous were delighted with Benedict's plans for their house and the building work began. The Du Plicitous family moved into a suite at the Ritz while their butler, Ernest, lived in the house to keep an eye on everything and to look after their cat, Chiang Mai. Ernest, unlike his employers, was very nice, and he and Norma soon became quite friendly.

One particularly hot Friday afternoon, Violet and Rose were walking home from school with Norma. As they passed the Du Plicitous house they nearly walked straight into Isabella, who was getting out of an enormous limousine with blacked-out windows. The door was being held open for her by Ernest, who looked delighted to see Norma.

Violet remembered her mother's words from the night she had met Isabella, and said hello politely and introduced Rose.

Isabella looked at them both as if they were nasty worms and didn't reply. Instead she said in an irritable voice, 'Hurry up, Ernest! Let's get inside quickly.'

'Yes, of course, Miss Isabella,' he replied, sprinting up the stairs to the house to open the front door.

Violet stuck out her tongue at Isabella's back, making Rose laugh. They were about to walk on when curiosity got the better of Violet.

'I didn't think your family were living here yet,' she called after Isabella. 'And why are you home from boarding school?'

'We're not living here, I'm just doing something important for my parents,' Isabella answered without turning around. 'You should learn to mind your own business, nosy!'

Rose and Violet exchanged glances. Norma frowned but said nothing.

Later that evening, Violet was roaming around the house, moaning that she was too hot to sleep and generally getting on Norma's nerves. Norma was babysitting because Violet's father was away for work and Camille was out for dinner.

'It's too late to play with Rose, but why don't you go and see Dee Dee?' Norma suggested. 'You can take her some of the prawns left over from supper.' Norma worried about Dee Dee's diet and so was always sending over dishes of proper food with Violet.

Violet nodded enthusiastically, thinking that she would like to see Dee Dee and also that she might have something cooling and yummy in her freezer like mint-choc-chip ice cream. So Violet went off, clutching a container of food, Norma's strict instructions to be back in twenty minutes ringing in her ears.

The garden was quiet and almost empty in the dusk. Lydia's older sister, Beatrice, and

Tom were sitting on a bench talking, and they waved to Violet as she passed them. Reaching Dee Dee's flat, Violet knocked on the door. There was no answer. All the lights were off, although one of the windows was wide open.

Violet had just decided that Dee Dee must be out and was about to leave, when she saw a light flash inside the flat, like a torch being flicked on and off. *That's strange*, Violet thought, and knocked on the door again, calling out to Dee Dee. But again there was no answer, so Violet turned and left.

Beatrice and Tom had gone by now, but as she crossed the garden once more, Violet spotted Pudding and Lullabelle on the other side of

the lawn. She went and stroked the cats for a while, sitting on the cool, green grass. While she was there, an arrogant-looking Siamese cat swaggered past them, his nose in the air. *This must be Chiang-Mai*, thought Violet, *he looks as stuckup as his owners.*

It was nearly dark by now, so Violet headed for home. But then she saw something very strange. At first she thought she must be seeing things in the gloomy light, so she stopped and looked properly.

Now she could clearly see a small, dark figure climbing up the drainpipe at the back of the Count's house. Violet ran over to get a better look, but the climber was so fast that by the time Violet reached the house he had disappeared.

How peculiar! Violet thought. *Why would anyone be climbing up the Count's drainpipe?*

'Violet, come on!' Norma called, peering out of the back door and looking thunderous. Violet scampered over to her, deciding not to mention what she had seen in case she got into even more trouble for spying.

'She wasn't there,' she announced, returning the prawns to Norma.

The following morning, Violet slept late. When she woke up, she wandered into the bathroom. It was thick with steam and smelt deliciously of lilac. Her mother was lying in the bath, her hair wrapped in an emerald-green turban, drinking a tiny cup of coffee.

'Good morning, cherie. How are you, my darling? I cannot believe you slept through all the noise and kerfuffle last night.'

'What noise? What happened?' Violet asked.

'Dee Dee was burgled while she was out at the theatre. When I came back from dinner, the whole garden was crawling with police.' Violet's mother sighed. 'It is really terrible news because they took an incredibly valuable brooch. I know the Countess said Dee Dee had an impressive jewel but I had no idea she meant such an expensive piece. And I cannot believe that Dee Dee kept it in her flat; it should have been in the bank.'

'You don't mean the Pearl of the Orient?'

'Yes! How on earth do you know about it?' her mother asked, looking amazed.

'Because Dee Dee lets me wear it when I go round there, for dressing up. She keeps it in her biscuit tin.'

Camille made a face of horrified disbelief, accompanied by a sharp intake of breath. 'You know that is one of the largest pearls ever found. It has been missing for years, and the whole time it was being kept in a biscuit tin?' Violet's mother drained her cup of coffee. 'In any case, poor Dee Dee is very upset so maybe you should go over and see her later.'

But Violet wasn't really listening, she was thinking. The flash of light in Dee Dee's flat, the climbing figure – of course! The burglar! She told her mother what she had seen.

'Cherie,' Camille announced decisively, stepping daintily out of the bath and wrapping herself in an emerald-green towel. 'We must tell the police immediately. I think they will still be with Dee Dee, so quickly, let us get dressed and we will go to her flat.'

One policeman was still with Dee Dee.
His name was PC Green and he was young
and enthusiastic. He hadn't actually solved
a crime yet, but was very, very keen to try.

Poor Dee Dee sat in an armchair, with a face
like a pale, deflated balloon, and tears pouring
down her face. Violet and her mother were
a little surprised to see the Count there,
but Dee Dee was quick to say how marvellous
and helpful he had been.

'It is the least I can do, dear lady,' the

Count said, his face the picture of concern. 'I cannot help but feel a little guilty. If only I had not given you that theatre ticket then none of this might have happened.'

'Nonsense,' Dee Dee protested. 'Guilty about giving me the best ticket in the house, to see the greatest show in town? Don't be ridiculous. It was incredibly kind and generous of you.'

By the window, PC Green was holding up something to the light in his gloved hands, examining it carefully. The Count rushed over to him.

'Have you found a clue?' Camille asked.

Violet went over to see what they were looking at.

'Possibly,' PC Green answered thoughtfully. 'A couple of long red hairs caught in the window frame. They might belong to the burglar.'

'Hmm, perhaps,' the Count said quickly. 'But, PC Green, and forgive me if I am speaking out of turn, but haven't you noticed Mrs Derota also has long red hair?'

PC Green sighed. 'Of course, silly me.'

'But Dee Dee's hair is lighter and more coppery than that,' Violet said. 'and also it's not as long, and—'

She was about to go on, but the Count interrupted her curtly. 'Violet, are you now

HAIR

adding amateur detective to your many skills?' he asked her in a not very nice way, a fake smile pinned to his face.

Camille answered for her. 'Well, in fact Violet does think that she may have some other information that will help find the burglar.'

Both the Count and PC Green looked up sharply. Even Dee Dee looked a little perkier.

'Last night, at about nine o'clock, Violet was in the garden when she saw—'

But before Camille could continue, the Count rushed to Dee Dee's side.

'Dear lady,' he cried, 'You look so pale suddenly. Are you feeling faint?'

Dee Dee was taken aback at his expression of alarm. 'Er, well, I do feel a little shaken.'

'You do look a bit under the weather, ma'am,' the policeman said thoughtfully. 'It must have been a terrible shock – shall we get the doctor to look you over?'

Camille nodded. 'I think it might be sensible.'

'We should call an ambulance,' the Count quickly suggested.

'Leave it to me,' PC Green announced, with the air of a man who could sort such things out easily. He started talking into his walkie-talkie in his important police language. 'Bravo, Lima, Delta calling. Immediate request for an ambulance to 15 Melrose Crescent, Whisky, Tango, Foxtrot. Over and out.'

Seconds later, there was a blare of sirens, a whirl of blue lights and a rap on the door. Dee Dee looked slightly bemused as two young men bustled in and started talking to her as if she were about two years old. Still, she allowed herself to be helped out to the ambulance.

'I do think one of us should go with her, just in case,' the Count said, still looking concerned. 'Alas, I have an important prior engagement with Isabella. She returned from boarding school this morning to stay with us for the weekend and she would so disappointed if I cancelled.

Camille, would you mind terribly going with Mrs Derota?' He stared imploringly at Violet's mother.

That's a lie, Violet thought. *Isabella came back yesterday. Rose and I saw her on our way back from school.*

'Of course not,' said Camille. 'Violet, please tell PC Green what you saw and then go straight home to Norma. Tell your father where I have gone.' She scurried after Dee Dee and the ambulance disappeared in another whirlwind of sirens and flashing blue lights.

'So Violet, what exactly did you see?' PC Green asked kindly, pen poised above his notepad.

'Well, it was about nine o'clock last night,' Violet began hesitantly. 'And I came into the garden to come and see Dee Dee—'

'Do you normally go wandering around the garden at night, Violet?' asked the Count. The kind concern had gone from his face.

'No,' said Violet blushing. 'But I was too hot to sleep and I thought Dee Dee might have some mint-choc-chip ice cream.'

PC Green smiled and Violet continued, ending her account with the small figure climbing up the drainpipe.

'What, like Spiderman?' queried the Count, his voice heavy with disbelief. 'Are you sure you have not been watching too much television, Violet dear?' He raised his eyebrows at PC Green as if to say, *Do you really believe this nonsense?* Then he began to speak in his most oily voice. 'Detective Inspector Green...'

'Er, just PC at the moment, Count,' the young man protested, clearly flattered.

'My apologies, I am sure you will soon be climbing the ranks. Did I mention my friendship with the Chief Inspector? Such a charming man ... but where was I? Oh yes, the drainpipe,' he smiled his fake smile. 'Come with me, PC Green, let us look at this drainpipe.'

They all trooped outside and in the clear morning light, the drainpipe looked very old and rickety. The Count gave it a tug and the whole thing practically came away from the wall.

'I don't think any burglar is going to be climbing that, do you?' said the Count, looking triumphantly at the policeman.

'No, I wouldn't have thought that it would hold anyone heavier than a child,' PC Green agreed.

'And what child would possibly go around stealing precious jewels?' the Count added quickly.

'But I saw someone,' Violet protested crossly, her face reddening.

'The imagination is a powerful thing, Violet,' PC Green said earnestly.

'Such words of wisdom, PC Green. The Police Inspector must hear of your talent.' The Count shook the policeman's hand warmly. And, without saying anything to Violet, he walked off.

'Right, Violet, let's get you home,' PC Green announced, steering her back towards Dee Dee's flat.

'Where are we going? We can just walk across the garden,' said Violet.

'Where's the fun in that?' cried PC Green.

'Wouldn't you rather have a ride in my squad car? I can put the sirens and lights on.' The policeman looked so excited at the thought of this that Violet didn't like to spoil his fun. She followed him through Dee Dee's flat and out to the street.

However, PC Green couldn't quite remember where he had parked his car and while he was wandering up and down the street trying to find it, Violet spotted the Count standing on the opposite side of the road, talking intently to a man in a parked van. She crouched down between two cars, trying to get a better look without being seen. The Count glanced around nervously, as if he were worried about being watched, then handed the driver a small package. As soon as he had done so, he ran across the road and climbed into a waiting limousine that immediately drove off. The van then drove off too, past Violet. She noticed *F. Orger*, written on the side of it. Why did that name sound so familiar?

But before Violet could wrack her brains, PC Green walked back to her, looking very worried. 'I think that someone has stolen my car!'

Violet scanned the street. 'Isn't that it?' she said, pointing to a police car parked a little way down the road.

'Yes! How silly am I? That would have been the third time this week I'd reported it stolen when it was parked right under my nose.'

The car was very messy and Violet had to move a book and a pile of papers from the back seat so she could sit down.

INVESTIGATING CRIME THE SCIENTIFIC WAY

BY SHIRLEY SOLVIT

'That's an amazing book – I've just finished it,' said PC Green looking at the book in her hand. 'It only took me six months,' he added proudly.

Violet's mind was whirring with ideas. 'May I borrow it?'

PC Green looked pleased. 'Of course. Now, Violet, shall we have some fun?' And with a huge grin he turned on the lights and siren and they drove the short distance to Violet's house at top speed.

6
THE CRIME SOLVING MATRIX

The following week was a rather trying one in the Remy-Robinson household. It was still very hot and although the weather forecast kept saying that it would rain, it never did. The sky just got darker and darker, the air stickier and stickier, and everyone got hotter and grumpier. Benedict was away until Thursday and Camille was working very hard designing the last few pieces of jewellery for her new collection.

And Violet? Well, the matter of the

climbing figure and the missing jewel refused to stop rattling around her head. She knew she had seen someone in the garden, and she couldn't understand why the Count had lied about Isabella's return from boarding school and why he been so dismissive of her witness account. It was as if he didn't want PC Green to believe a word she said, as if he didn't want Dee Dee's jewel to be found.

Violet spent most of her spare time in the garden with Rose discussing the crime, as it was the most exciting thing to have happened in a long time. There were two things that they were particularly concerned about.

Number One was Dee Dee. The doctors

at the hospital had decided that the old lady should spend the week there and both Rose's mother, Maeve, and Camille had been to visit her. They didn't say much to the girls, but from overheard snippets of conversation the pair gleaned that Dee Dee was still very upset by the theft and not at all well.

Number Two was PC Green. Was a policeman who managed to lose his car three times in a week really likely to be able to solve a difficult crime such as this? Sure enough, it was only Thursday when Camille received a phone call from PC Green asking her to tell Dee Dee that he was very sorry but he was intending to close the case due to lack of evidence.

'But he can't just do that!' Violet exclaimed, when her mother told her.

'I agree, *chérie*, it is upsetting. I think I won't tell Dee Dee until she has fully recovered.'

'But there are clues! What about the red hair? What about the climbing figure that I saw?'

Camille shrugged. 'I'm sorry, Violet. Now I must get on with some work. Why don't you go and find Rose?'

So that was exactly what Violet did, clutching PC Green's crime book in her hand.

Later that night, Violet lay in bed, unable to sleep. *How could anyone sleep*, she thought, *when they had just discovered the identity* of a major criminal? She switched on her bedside light for the umpteenth time to look at the 'crime solving matrix' she and Rose had written, as instructed in PC Green's book.

However, there was one major problem. No one believed them. When Violet and Rose

CRIME TO SOLVE: THE THEFT OF MRS DEROTA'S JEWEL, KNOWN AS THE PEARL OF THE ORIENT

<u>WHERE DID THE CRIME TAKE PLACE?</u>
DEE DEE'S FLAT, WHILE SHE WAS OUT AT THE THEATRE.
TICKET BOUGHT BY THE COUNT DU PLICITOUS!

<u>WERE THERE ANY WITNESSES TO THE CRIME?</u>
YES, VIOLET REMY-ROBINSON

<u>IF SO, WHAT DID THEY SEE?</u>
A TORCH FLASHING IN THE FLAT AND THEN
A FIGURE CLIMBING UP THE BACK OF THE BUILDING.

<u>WHAT CLUES WERE THERE?</u>
LONG RED HAIR CAUGHT IN THE WINDOW.
WHAT CONCLUSIONS CAN BE DRAWN FROM THIS?
THE THIEF HAS LONG RED HAIR AND IS A GOOD CLIMBER

<u>WHAT CONCLUSIONS CAN BE DRAWN FROM THIS?</u>
THE THIEF HAS LONG RED HAIR AND IS A GOOD CLIMBER.

showed the matrix to Norma, she looked concerned and confused. It was a very 'serious matter', Norma said, to accuse someone of stealing. That was also what Violet's mother said, looking rather less concerned and confused, and more certain, that the Count

DO THESE DETAILS MATCH ANY SUSPECTS?
YES! ISABELLA DU PLICITIOUS!!!!

IF SO, DO THEY HAVE AN ALIBI?
NOT KNOWN. ROSE AND VIOLET SAW HER IN THE AFTERNOON, AND THEN, BUT THE COUNT LIED ABOUT HER NOT RETURNING FROM BOARDING SCHOOL UNTIL THE NEXT DAY. VERY SUSPICIOUS.

DO THEY HAVE A MOTIVE?
YES; TO STEAL THE PEARL OF THE ORIENT FOR HER GREEDY, HORRIBLE PARENTS.

DOES THIS LEAD YOU TO A SENSIBLE CONCLUSION?
YES!! ISABELLA IS THE THIEF!

CONGRATULATIONS, YOU HAVE SOLVED THE CRIME!

and Countess would never be involved in such a thing, let alone their daughter. And it was also what Benedict said, when he arrived back from his trip, although he wasn't at all concerned or confused, just absolutely convinced that Violet and Rose were wrong, and a bit cross that they would suggest it. Rose tried showing the matrix to her parents too but they made almost identical comments.

Of course, none of this shook the girls' absolute belief in their theory, but they could see that much as they loved their parents and Norma dearly, they were going to be of no use at all in getting back Dee Dee's jewel.

It was clear to Violet as she lay in her bed that evening that she, Violet Remy-Robinson, would have to take matters into her own hands (with, hopefully, some help from Rose). Her first step would be to go and see PC Green the very next day. As a policeman surely he would take their deductions seriously?

VIOLET'S
SCHOOL

7

Escape from
St Catherine's

By a stroke of luck, Violet and Rose's school,
St Catherine's, was located just a couple
of streets away from the police station, so
it seemed obvious to Violet that by far the
simplest way to see PC Green was to slip out
of school. But, of course, this was far easier
said than done, as St Catherine's was very
keen on security. There were entry phones,
buzzers, locked gates and bolted doors at every
turn. And not so much, Violet often thought,
to keep people out, but to keep the children in.

Escaping would be a little like escaping from prison.

Violet met Rose the following morning before school for an emergency pow-wow in the quietest corner of the school cloakroom. By then Violet had already thought, plotted and pondered, coming up with three plans. As Violet explained them, Rose's eyebrows drew together in a concerned knot, because as much as Rose wanted to help, she couldn't help but think of the terrible telling-off they would get if they were caught.

Despite Rose's concerns, there was no time to waste, so that very morning, Violet attempted Plan A.

PLAN A

striding straight forwardly and brazenly out of the front door.

'I have to go to the dentist,' Violet announced with total confidence to her form teacher, Miss Tucker, after the first lesson.

Miss Tucker looked surprised. 'I don't have any record of that in the register. Did your parents tell the school?'

'Oh, yes, definitely. I brought the note in and gave it to the school secretary myself.'

Miss Tucker thought for a moment. Violet was usually honest and trustworthy. 'Okay,' she replied. 'You'd better go downstairs and

82

wait for your mother in the hall.'

Violet nodded, grabbed her coat and darted out the door before Miss Tucker could change her mind. Rose mouthed 'good luck' to her as Violet passed her desk.

Miss Brisk, the school secretary and guardian of the buzzer to the front door, was on the telephone. Violet waited for her to finish, hopping from one foot to the other, as she sometimes did when she was nervous. And then, just as Miss Brisk was putting down the phone, something deeply annoying happened. The headmistress, Mrs Rumperbottom, came out of her office. Her beady eyes fixed upon Violet.

'Violet,' she said suspiciously. 'How can we help? Shouldn't you be in class?'

Violet's courage took a large dip. She hadn't reckoned on dealing with scary Mrs Rumperbottom.

'Well, you see, I think, I mean, I am meant to be going to the dentist, and er . . .' She could feel herself going pink as she began to stumble through her carefully rehearsed lie.

Mrs Rumperbottom held up her hand for silence. 'Miss Brisk, do you have a letter from Violet's parents about a trip to the dentist?'

Miss Brisk shook her head. 'No, Headmistress, I'm afraid not.'

'I see,' Mrs Rumperbottom replied slowly,

drawing out each syllable. 'It appears, Violet, that you are mistaken. You will not be going to the dentist today, so I suggest that you return to your classroom as quickly as your little legs will carry you.' And Violet had no choice but to abandon Plan A and stomp back up the stairs to her classroom.

At breaktime, Violet and Rose tried Plan B.

PLAN B

Sneaking out of the kitchen with Rose distracting Mrs Macstew, the school cook, as necessary.

Dorothy MacStew, the school cook, was nearly as fierce as Mrs Rumperbottom, so the two girls approached the kitchen door with some nervousness. First break happened to coincide with the daily food deliveries, and, as they gingerly pushed open the swing doors, they could hear Mrs MacStew shouting at the butcher.

The poor man stood with his head bowed, as she lectured him on the many faults his sausages displayed. He was delighted to see the small figure of Rose coming towards them, interrupting his telling-off.

Rose positioned herself so that Mrs MacStew was facing away from the back door and began to nervously deliver her speech about her mother having decided that Rose was allergic to gluten so could she have a special lunch, please?

Mrs MacStew seemed to find this extremely irritating, but both she and the butcher were so distracted they didn't notice Violet creep towards the back door.

Yes! Violet thought. *This is going to work!*

But just at that moment, the baker arrived at the back door, as he too had been summoned for a good telling-off about his rolls. He rang the bell, and Mrs MacStew looked over to the door.

'Violet!' she bellowed.

Violet froze and slowly turned around, ready with explanations. But Mrs MacStew wasn't interested. 'Get back to the playground! And you too, Rose! Please tell your mother that if she wants you to be gluttenous free she will have to send in a packed lunch!'

Disastrous. That was the only word to describe the escape attempts so far. So Rose and Violet went into a huddle in the playground and contemplated the tricky and dangerous nature of Plan C.

'Are you sure this is a good idea?' Rose asked Violet anxiously.

Violet paused before answering, as she too was feeling less than sure. But then she

ALLEY

PLAN C

EEK!

WALL

STAFF ROOM

CLASS 1

CLASS 2

FIRE ESCAPE

TOILET

WINDOW

DINNER HALL

STAIRS

ART ROOM

thought of Dee Dee and nodded with all the enthusiasm she could muster.

After they had finished their art lesson, the two girls hid themselves in the toilet, listening to the rest of their class hurtle down the stairs towards the dining room for lunch. When all was quiet, Violet eased up the toilet window and climbed out, with Rose gripping tightly onto her upper arms as she lowered herself down onto the rusty old fire escape. Violet whispered goodbye, then ran as quietly as she could down to the first floor of the building.

Bleep bleep. The alarm on Violet's watch sounded, warning her that lunch finished in two minutes.

Oh no, she thought, *I'm taking too long.*

And she had just reached the really tricky bit – getting from the fire escape to the high wall by the alley. And the gap was much wider than she had thought.

Holding onto the fire escape railings, Violet stretched out as far as she could, but she was still a way off. She couldn't jump – it would be impossible not to lose her balance. But there was no time to go back, and in a minute everyone would finish lunch and she would be found, clinging to the back of the building. She began to panic. How could she reach just a bit further? And then, looking down and seeing her school tie, Violet had a brainwave. Quick as a flash, she untied it from her neck and knotted it around the railings. Grasping the tie, she leaned right out and s-t-r-e-t-c-h-i-n-g as far as she could she just managed to step safely onto the wall. The lunch bell rang out and everyone flooded into the playground, just as Violet lowered herself down into the alley and scampered off towards the police station.

PC Green seemed to have been promoted; he had a smart office and Violet noticed that everyone was calling him Inspector Green. He was delighted to see her, or, to be more accurate, was delighted until she showed

him the crime-solving matrix when a cloud seemed to settle over the policeman's face. Before Violet had finished explaining, he interrupted her brusquely.

'Violet, I have to tell you that I find your accusations against the Du Plicitous family quite preposterous.' Violet tried to protest but he held up his hand to quieten her, his face reddening with anger. 'I could spend hours telling you how wrong you and your matrix are, but I haven't the time because I have lots of important police work to do. So I will just say that the main reason that it is all totally ridiculous is that this very morning the Count came to see me to say that he had found the Pearl of the Orient in a flowerbed outside Mrs Derota's flat and had returned it safely to her. So, Violet, what do you think of that?' he challenged triumphantly.

Violet was so amazed by this news that she didn't know what to say. But that didn't matter because there was a polite tap on the door. A young policewoman appeared.

'Sorry to bother you, Sir, but I thought you might be interested to know that

St Catherine's has just reported a missing pupil,' she said, looking pointedly at Violet.

'Oh dear, Violet,' PC Green smirked, full of mock sympathy. 'You seem to be in rather a lot of trouble, don't you?'

8

GODMOTHER CELESTE AND OTHER SUMMER TREATS

It was a little before midnight when Violet finally stopped crying and fell asleep.

Camille had had to leave work to collect Violet from the police station, and the memory of her mother's concerned, embarrassed face was enough to make Violet prickle with guilt. Mrs Rumperbottom had met them at the police station and told Camille how horrified she was by Violet's escape and that she would be suspending her from school. And worse still, Mrs MacStew had told on Rose, and she too was to be suspended for helping Violet. Since term ended the following week, the school had no wish to see either of them until September.

Benedict had been waiting when they got home, looking very angry. Apparently the Count had already heard about Violet's accusations – no doubt from PC Green, Violet thought – and had rung her father up, shouting so loudly that Benedict had had to hold the telephone away from his ear. The Count had ranted about how deeply offended he was to be suspected of such a thing, saying that he had a good mind to fire Benedict. If there were any further accusations he would make sure

Benedict never worked again. Violet's parents were so upset that they had asked her to write a long, grovelling letter of apology to the Du Plicitouses.

Only Norma had been of any comfort. She had made Violet tomato and cheese pizza for supper and later, when she brought Violet some hot milk to help her sleep. 'Mrs Derota is a very nice lady and your friend,' she said kindly, giving Violet's arm a gentle squeeze. 'You tried to help her; nothing wrong with that.' But Violet wouldn't listen, and she cried and cried.

It was unfortunate that Violet wasn't aware until later the next day that Mrs

Rumperbottom's visit to Rose's house hadn't worked out quite as the headmistress had expected. It might have made Violet feel better.

Rose and her mother, who was rather like an older version of Rose, had seen Mrs Rumperbottom coming up the stairs to the house and had hidden in the bathroom. Therefore, it was Rose's father who answered the door to the headmistress. Robert Trelawney was a very successful lawyer and so, fresh from court and still dressed in his wig and gown, he demanded to know the case against his daughter and when it was presented to him, he was most unimpressed.

'As a criminal barrister, Mrs Rumperbottom,

I am a man who deals in hard facts and proper evidence and not what I would call, at best, flimsy assumptions. It would appear, Mrs Rumperbottom, that you are proposing to suspend my daughter for asking Mrs MacStew for a gluten-free lunch, which is not, as far as I'm aware, a crime – if it were, surely half of England would be in jail? Now am I missing something?'

It was not often that Mrs Rumperbottom was at a loss for words. In fact, she was so stunned that when she did open her mouth and try to speak, no words would come out. Rose's father held the front door open and ushered her out.

'I'm delighted you agree with me,' he said. 'So you'll be seeing Rose tomorrow morning as usual. A pleasure as ever, Mrs Rumperbottom. Do call again whenever you wish. Good night.' And he slammed the door.

The next morning, Violet's godmother, Celeste, arrived to stay between visiting the Chilean Salt Plains and the Norwegian Fjords. On seeing everyone's grave faces, and Violet's red puffy eyes, she asked what on earth the matter was. She listened to the tale solemnly, but when it was over, a slight smile could be seen lurking around her mouth.

'Oh, dear. It sounds terribly serious,' she

said, in a tone of voice that implied she didn't think that it was serious at all. 'But I also think it displays a certain spirit and a sense of justice in Violet and Rose, which are both very good character traits.' She gave Violet a crafty wink. 'And, as far as school goes, at least Violet was not expelled from the school for doing something really, really bad like locking her geography teacher in the stationary cupboard for six whole hours, so the poor woman nearly had a nervous breakdown, *n'est-ce pas,* Camille?'

For some reason which Violet didn't understand, her mother went bright red and gave Celeste a furious look.

This made Celeste smile even more and Benedict gave a guffaw of laughter. At that moment, Norma walked in with a tray piled high with bacon and waffles for breakfast and a good mood was restored in the Remy-Robinson household.

Celeste pulled a bottle of champagne out of her backpack.

'I feel a toast is called for.' *Pop!* The cork exploded and a fountain of fizz was slopped into the grown- ups' glasses, with just a splash added to Violet's orange juice. 'Ladies and gentlemen, please raise your glasses to a glorious summer, to the return of Mrs Derota's brooch – which will hopefully now be kept in the bank rather than the biscuit tin – and to Violet, who didn't get expelled from school, only suspended, unlike—' But Celeste couldn't continue, because Camille had firmly clamped her hand over her mouth.

Much to Violet's delight, Celeste stayed for a few days by the end of which the summer holidays had truly begun and Violet's school breakout had been entirely forgiven by her parents. As usual, every minute of Violet's holidays was accounted for, and her timetable looked something like this:

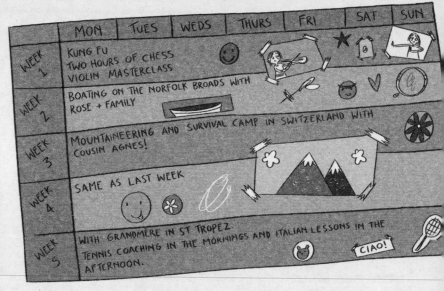

At this point, I could launch into many tales of Violet's boating adventures with Rose, and how she came to push Stanley off the boat practically every day, and why she and naughty Cousin Agnes ended up spending a night alone up a mountain with only a few goats for company, or what terrible trouble they got into with Grandmère over a pot of raspberry jam, but there is not really the time or the space, and, more to the point, it would have nothing to do with Dee Dee, the Count, or the Pearl of the Orient. So there will be a brief interruption in our story, for I'm afraid that it does not end here with the safe return of the brooch to Dee Dee. Oh no, the drama will recommence in September . . .

'Violet and Rose, my darlings! I am so dee-lighted to see you! Don't you both look brown as berries and just as scrumptious?' Dee Dee cried as the girls appeared on her doorstep in early September. Violet was clutching several dishes of food and an enormous Toblerone. 'Oh, and you have come bearing edible gifts. How wonderful! And Swiss chocolate! My favourite. Come in, come in.'

Dee Dee's flat was as messy as ever. Lullabelle was lying on a pile of clothes in the

middle of the floor and Violet had to remove
several odd shoes from a chair in order to
sit down.

'I have discovered these delicious cakes,' Dee
Dee said, producing a plate of French Fancies.
'They are so yummy and light, and look how
pretty they are. You must try one.' They all
munched and chatted away about the holidays
and the summer. Then Dee Dee told the girls
of her plans for the Pearl of the Orient.

'I have decided to sell it,' she announced

with a broad beam. 'It brings me no pleasure now that it is sitting in the bank. Besides, the Count has told me he wants to increase my rent by rather a lot, and, girls, I can tell you that retired Hollywood actresses do not get a good pension. So thank goodness I have the Pearl to pay for my old age. Violet, please thank your mother for recommending a jewellery specialist to me. She sounds so nice and I have an appointment to see her tomorrow. Now I just need to decide what I am going to wear.'

'That's great, Dee Dee. I hope you get a good price for it.' Violet said.

'Oh, I'm sure I will. I'm in the money!' Dee

Dee hummed happily to herself. 'Now, what do you think my darlings, shall I wear the canary-yellow chiffon or the aubergine crepe?'

'Aubergine crepe,' Violet and Rose said at the same time.

'Most definitely,' Violet added, just to be clear. 'Thank you for the cakes, Dee Dee, but I should probably go home for supper.'

'Me too,' agreed Rose.

'All right, my darlings. You have a good evening and see you soon. Be sure to thank Norma for her delicious food – she is such a fabulous cook, and a sweetheart of a lady.'

The girls walked out into the autumn sunshine, both thinking the same thing.

Thank goodness that the Pearl of the Orient had been safely returned to Dee Dee. Imagine if she didn't have the jewel to sell - what would become of her?

The following evening, Violet was just finishing her violin practice when her mother arrived home. This was highly unusual as it was only five o'clock. Camille, looked very worried, went into the study to talk to Benedict and then announced that she had to go out again.

Six-thirty came and went without Camille's return, and Benedict stayed in his study, talking in a low voice on the telephone. Violet hovered around outside the door, desperately trying to overhear something. Then her father appeared and went straight out into the garden, looking very distracted.

What on earth was going on? Violet felt itchy with excitement, but also nervous in case it was something bad. It was not until later when Benedict came to say goodnight to her that she found out.

'Your mother is with Dee Dee,' he explained.

'She is terribly upset, because, as it turns out, her brooch is a fake. A very good fake, but a fake.'

Violet's jaw dropped. 'Dave Derota would not have bought Dee Dee a fake jewel; he loved her, even more than Marilyn,' she said defensively.

This made her father smile a little, despite the circumstances.

'I'm sure Dave loved her very much and had no idea that it was a fake,' he said. 'But it is, darling. Your mother has looked at it, as has another jewellery specialist. It is disastrous news for Dee Dee. I know that she told you and Rose about the Count raising her rent enormously. But I am sure he will be fair and give her a couple of months to find somewhere else to live. We can all help her to move.'

Violet's eyes began to well up with tears. 'But that's Dee Dee's home, she shouldn't have to move, it's not fair! The Count is rich enough already, why does he need more money? I bet it's because he still wants to turn her lovely flat into a swimming pool! Remember he asked her to leave when he first arrived—'

'Ssshh, don't get upset, darling. I know it seems unfair but unfortunately this is the way the world works.'

'Well, it's wrong,' Violet fumed. 'I want to

see Dee Dee.' She started to get out of bed.

'No, no,' her father insisted. 'She is very upset, Violet and she wouldn't want you to see her like that. Your mother is sitting with her. It's better if you go and see her tomorrow. You go to sleep now. Night night.' He stroked her cheek.

Violet kissed him goodnight, feeling thoroughly cross and wondering how she could help Dee Dee with this new piece of bad luck.

The following day was a Saturday, and after an early morning emergency meeting with Rose, the girls got to work raising money for Dee Dee. They set up a lemonade and cupcake stand in the garden which did a roaring trade and by the end of the day, they had a jam jar full of coins which they counted out carefully. Twenty-two pounds and ninety-four pence. It seemed like an enormous sum of money. Surely it would help Dee Dee pay her rent?

So when Violet knocked on Dee Dee's door,

with the jar of
money and a box of
French Fancies, she
was feeling pretty
hopeful. But then
Dee Dee came to
the door, looking
very different from

normal. She had no makeup on and her hair
was up in a messy bun. Violet could not believe
how old and tired she looked as she took the
cakes and the jar with the faintest of smiles.

'Do you mind, sweetheart, if I don't invite
you in? I'm kinda tired. Here, you must take
a cake though. Thank you so much for them

and the money. I'll miss you so much when . . .' she trailed off, her eyes filling with tears. 'I've gotta go, honey, but will you come and see me another day, when I'm feeling more myself?'

Violet nodded, too upset to speak. She had hardly ever seen a grown-up cry and it made her feel very sad. Dee Dee shut the door and Violet went back up the stairs to the garden. The Count and Countess had moved into their newly renovated house and the lights were all on. The Countess's horrible donkey laugh rang out from an open window on the first floor. Fury filled Violet, like water pouring into a cup. How dare they laugh when they were making Dee Dee so unhappy?

She found herself climbing up the oak tree, not caring that it was forbidden.

The leaves on the tree hid Violet completely, but there were enough gaps to allow her a clear view into the Count's magnificent dining room. Dinner was being served by Ernest, who was zooming around the table, dressed like a waiter in a fancy

restaurant and bearing silver platters.

'Coraline, my love,' the Count's voice wafted out to Violet as she watched him raise his glass to the Countess, who was draped in a gold silk dress that matched the curtains.

'Renard, my Count,' she replied, taking a sip from her glass. 'I cannot tell you how much I adore my gorgeous little gift from you.'

And she stroked something on her chest that Violet couldn't see.

'I think we should toast our brilliant friend Mr Frederick Orger too, don't you? Without whom, I would have no gift and we would not be able to build our magnificent new basement swimming pool!' They both cackled away.

That name again, Violet thought. It was the name from the van and from somewhere else too. If only she could remember. Just then, Violet heard a rustling beneath her and looked down to see a familiar head climbing up the tree beneath her. That was all she needed.

'Oi, Vileness, whatya doing?' Stanley cooed in his annoying voice. 'I hope you're not spying.'

'Shut up and go away!' she hissed as he climbed up next to her.

'Wow! You can see right into their house,' he whispered.

Rose chose that moment to appear at the bottom of the tree.

'Both of you come down now. It's really dangerous!' she called up anxiously.

'*Ssshhh!!!*' they both chorused.

But it was too late. The Countess stopped laughing and froze, listening intently.

'What is it, my love?' the Count asked, concerned, as his wife rose to her feet and strode over to the window.

'I heard voices,' she replied, peering out of

the window, her icy blue eyes fixed on the tree. Violet and Stanley shrank back against the trunk, trying to hide themselves.

'It will be the children playing in the garden, my sweetie pie,' the Count reassured her.

'No, it was closer than that,' the Countess replied and she brought the window down with a slam, just as Rose clambered up to the others.

'Come down now, please! What are you both staring at, anyway?' she asked, turning to the window.

'That is one ENORMOUS brooch she's got on,' Stanley said, as they stared transfixed at the jewel pinned to the Countess's chest.

'Isn't that— why on earth is she wearing the Pearl of the Orient?' Rose whispered to Violet.

'I don't know, but I think we had better find out,' Violet replied.

It was late and getting dark, but the girls had so much to discuss. What to do? A sleepover was the only answer, so they went and sweet-talked Rose's mother (who found saying no to anything very difficult). Five minutes later the girls were on their way back to Violet's, Rose clutching her pyjamas and toothbrush. As they walked into the sitting room, Violet stopped abruptly.

'Oh, Rose! I've remembered why I know that name, Mr Orger!' she cried. She went over to the mantelpiece, and produced the business card from behind the clock.

'He's the costume jewellery man the Countess recommended to my mother,' Violet explained to Rose. 'The Countess dropped this card when they were here for cocktails and I saw the Count talking to him outside Dee Dee's flat the day after the Pearl was stolen. The Du Plicitouses were toasting Mr Orger over dinner just now . . . but the Countess said that she never wore fake jewellery. I don't understand. What could he have done for them?' Violet felt as if the answer was staring her in the face, though she couldn't quite see it.

'I've got it,' Rose said softly. 'Violet, what if we were right all along and Isabella did steal the jewel for her parents? What if she gave it to her father and then the next day, when you saw him in the street, he was giving it to Mr Orger. He could have copied it, so there would be two jewels, identical to look at, but one real and one fake.'

Violet gasped. Rose had worked it out!

'Yes!' Violet gabbled as it all became clear. 'Then the Count pretended he'd found the jewel and instead of giving the *real* one back to Dee Dee he gave her the *fake* one. Dee Dee wouldn't have noticed the difference! It was only because she tried to sell it, that she found out its true value. That's it! Rose you are so clever!' Violet jumped up and down with excitement.

'Goodness!' Benedict exclaimed as he came

into the room. 'What are you so excited about?'

Violet, as ever, was about to blurt everything out to her father, but Rose stepped in quickly.

'It's a secret,' she said and quickly hurried Violet away. Because, as she said to her friend as they were cleaning their teeth, it would have been just like before. No one would believe them and the Count would just deny everything.

However scary it might be, if they wanted to get the Pearl of the Orient back they would have to do it themselves. So they told no one.

Well, actually that's not quite true, Violet did tell Norma. But Norma said nothing. Nothing at all. In fact, Violet wasn't even sure she was listening because she immediately changed the subject to talk about the weather.

Violet and Rose had had umpteen conversations about how to get Dee Dee's jewel back from the Du Plicitouses, but they had failed to come up with a really good plan. They were both beginning to think it might be impossible, but they couldn't bear to say it aloud to each other because whenever they saw Dee Dee she looked so miserable.

Then something happened.

A week or so after their sleepover, Violet came home from school to find a large black envelope, addressed to The Remy-Robinson Family in curly silver writing, sitting on the hall table.

It looks like a party invitation, she thought, *how exciting!*

And it was an invitation, but not to a party that Violet wanted to go to . . .

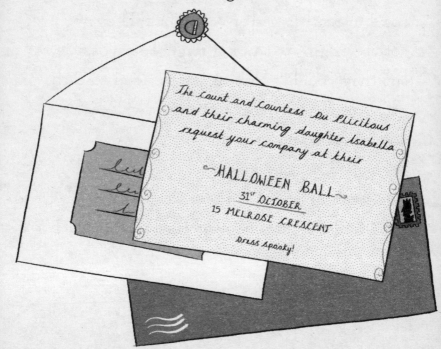

The count and Countess Du Plicikous
and their charming daughter Isabella
request your company at their

~HALLOWEEN BALL~
31ˢᵗ OCTOBER
15 MELROSE CRESCENT

Dress Spooky!

'We've had an invitation from the Count and Countess Du Plicitous and Isabella! How kind,' her mother said later, sipping her cocktail, the opened black envelope in her hand. 'Look, Violet, it is a Halloween party – does that mean we have to dress up?' she added, looking alarmed.

'I'm afraid so, darling,' Benedict replied, taking the invitation out of her hand and inspecting it before handing the card onto Violet.

Violet had no intention of going; she hated the Du Plicitouses for what they had done to Dee Dee and she was about to invent a new best friend at school who was having a Halloween party on the same night that she absolutely had to go to, when Norma said, almost as if she could read her mind, 'Violet, you must go. It will be fun. I will make you a lovely costume and you will get a chance to look round the house, and see how clever your father is at his work. Besides, Rose and some of the other children from the garden will probably be going.'

Violet was amazed because it was rare for Norma to say so much, and to sound so insistent.

'Okay, maybe,' Violet muttered. Perhaps, she thought, something would happen, like the Countess would be wearing the brooch and she could snatch it back off her. But even

Violet knew that wasn't really very likely.

Later Rose came over to tell her that her family had been invited too. Stanley was already going to another party, but her parents were keen to go. So both girls decided that whilst they'd rather be anywhere than at a Du Plicitous party, they would make the most of the occasion to search for clues.

Dee Dee was invited too but she politely declined, saying that she wasn't in a party mood.

'Happy Halloween! I am Count Dracula.' The Count greeted them at the door, his orange eyes gleaming. He was dressed in an

old fashioned white shirt and black suit, and his red hair was powdered white and greased back. His made-up face was deathly pale, with black rings around the eyes, and huge fangs dripping in fake blood protruding from his scarlet mouth.

'Good evening,' Camille replied, looking rather unnerved at his appearance. 'What amazing make-up, you really do make a very realistic vampire.' Violet's mother had done her best, putting on a black dress, a chic black wig and a little more black eye makeup than usual, but really she looked as elegant and unscary as ever.

This could not be said for the Countess

and Isabella, who jumped out at their guests and proceeded to do a rather odd, spooky dance in the hallway, clawing the air and hopping around like crazy cats. They were wearing matching black rubber catsuits with cut-out sections of red fishnet material, long, vivid red wigs, and a good deal of makeup.

Violet and her parents were stunned into silence for a moment, taking in the sight, until Benedict managed to stutter politely,' 'Er, don't you look two look . . . amazing!' He was dressed as a wizard but looked kind rather than scary.

Norma had been as good as her word and

made Violet a brilliant silver and gold skeleton costume. Isabella ran her eyes over it, a look of envy on her face.

'Doesn't the house look fabulously scary?' Camille exclaimed.

And it did. The only light came from dripping candelabras, and every shadowy inch was draped in cobwebs and black netting, with piles of pumpkins, skulls, and other spooky objects.

But the Count and Countess weren't listening to Camille's compliment. An enormous chauffeur-drive limousine had pulled up to the house.

'The Schnitzel von Doodlebugs have

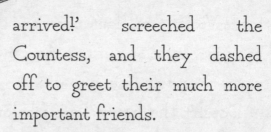

arrived!' screeched the Countess, and they dashed off to greet their much more important friends.

Violet spotted Rose and her parents in the hallway, standing near a person in a pumpkin suit who was holding a tray of drinks. Rose's family were dressed as zombies and greeted the Remy-Robinsons warmly. Camille and Benedict took a drink from the tray and as they turned away to speak to Rose's parents, the pumpkin handed Violet an origami witch's hat, with the words OPEN ME written on the front in glittery lettering.

Intrigued, Violet did so and, with Rose peering over her shoulder, began to read the words written inside.

!!TOP SECRET!!

Dear Violet and Rose,
This note holds instructions to help you retrieve the pearl of the orient. Tell no one and hide the note after reading!!
First, go and play with the other children at the party. The last game before supper will be sardines. Sneak off on your own and go to the Count and Countess's bedroom. Isabella will tell you it is locked and out of bounds. Be VERY careful no one sees you. The door will be unlocked for just a short time, so hurry! The jewel is in the safe at the back of the largest wardrobe and the safe combination is I-S-A-B-E-L-L-A
Shut the safe afterwards, hide the jewel in your pocket and come out and join the others. Be very quick and very quiet!

Good luck!
A Friend

'What have you got there, girls?' The Count's face loomed down over them. Rose cowered behind Violet.

'Oh, nothing. A note from a friend,' Violet replied, shoving the paper hat in her pocket.

'Well, run along then and join the other children, Isabella has some marvellous games planned,' he said, his eyes following them as they darted off.

Much to Violet and Rose's surprise they found themselves having a good time. Many of Isabella's friends were as poisonous as she was, but there were a couple of nice girls who had the misfortune to share Isabella's dormitory at boarding school. In fact, Violet was having such a good time apple bobbing and playing 'stick the tail on the devil' that it was only when Isabella announced that it was time to play sardines, and Rose gave her a big nudge with her elbow, that she remembered their secret mission.

'Now I'm going to hide,' Isabella announced bossily. 'I might be anywhere in the house, except my parents' bedroom suite on the first floor. That is locked because we are so rich and have so many valuable things, we just can't risk leaving it open,' she boasted. 'Now, shut your eyes and start counting!'

As soon as the game was in full swing, Rose and Violet hurried up to the first floor and tried the door to the bedroom. It wasn't locked! They opened it quietly, crept into

the moonlit room and over to the enormous wardrobe.

'You keep watch,' Violet whispered to Rose, who nodded in agreement. Then, feeling like Lucy about to find Narnia, Violet opened the wardrobe and pushed her way through the Countess's fur coats. The safe was at the back, just where the letter said it would be. It was shaped like a heart, which Violet hadn't expected. Yuck, how tacky, she thought as she punched the letters I-S-A-B-E-L-L-A into the keypad.

But instead of opening, the safe bleeped bossily and a message flashed up on the screen.

Violet was puzzled.

PASSWORD WRONG.
TWO MORE ATTEMPT LEFT
BEFORE ALARM SOUNDS.

'Rose!' she whispered. 'How do you spell Isabella?'

'I-S-A-B-E-L-L-A,' Rose replied. 'Please hurry up!' She was feeling so nervous that she thought she might explode.

Violet punched in the letters again. The safe gave another unfriendly bleep.

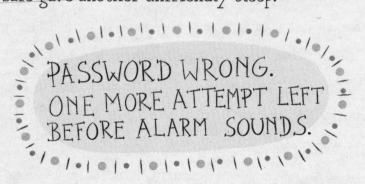

PASSWORD WRONG.
ONE MORE ATTEMPT LEFT
BEFORE ALARM SOUNDS.

Violet hesitated, unsure what to do. The password in the note must have been wrong.

But what else could it be?

Her thoughts were interrupted by Rose whispering to her, in a quavering voice, 'I think there's someone coming!'

Violet froze, because she too heard a pair of footsteps.

'What is the meaning of this?' roared a familiar male voice.

'I'm really, really s-s-sorry, M . . . Mr . . . Count . . . ' Rose stammered, sounding petrified.

Violet's heart began to thump.

'What are you doing in here?' he demanded furiously.

'Er, well,' Rose began. 'You see . . . I was . . . er . . . just looking for . . . for a friend of mine.'

'Which friend? Not Violet, by any chance?'

Violet shrank to the back of the cupboard.

'No, not Violet,' Rose squeaked. 'Absolutely, definitely not Violet. It was a new friend, called er . . . um . . . Esmeralda.' But the Count wasn't listening any more. He was pacing slowly round the bedroom, and Violet heard him stop in front of the wardrobe.

'Why is this wardrobe open?'

'Um . . . um . . . ' Rose stuttered.

But then another voice spoke.

'Renard!! What are you doing in here?' the Countess squawked. 'I need you downstairs this instant! Dinner is about to be served. Run along child!' she hissed at Rose.

Violet sensed hesitation from Rose before she heard a scurrying of feet.

The Count hesitated too.

'Come on, Renard! What are you waiting for?'

A moment's pause and then he said, 'Coming, my love.' Violet heard him pad out of the room, shutting and locking the door behind him.

Violet let out a long, slow, sweet sigh of relief, before realising that she was now locked in the Count's bedroom. She came out of the wardrobe and tried the door, just to be sure. Most definitely locked.

Downstairs the dinner gong sounded. Violet began to panic that she would shortly be missed and then the Count would come looking for her and then she would be in so much trouble and everyone would shout at her and . . .

Keep calm, she told herself firmly. She just needed to think; after all, there must be another way out. And of course, there was.

The sash window slid up quite smoothly. Violet climbed out, reaching for the rickety old drainpipe that PC Green had rattled, telling herself sternly, as her courage wavered, that it had supported Isabella climbing all the way up to the roof when she had stolen the Pearl of Orient, so it would support Violet on her short climb down to the ground.

Violet inched down the drainpipe as it wobbled, jumping the last bit and landing

softly on the grass. Violet tried to walk casually back into the house. But she bumped straight into the Count, his fangs gleaming in the moonlight.

'Violet! How funny, I was just talking about you with your little friend Rose. Where did you get to? Surely you weren't looking for Isabella outside?'

'Oh . . . yes! That's exactly what I was doing,' Violet replied, wide-eyed with innocence. 'I thought she might be in the garden shed.'

'What garden shed?' the Count asked sceptically.

'Oh, you know, the shed over there,'

Violet waved vaguely. 'Now I must go and find Rose . . .' She tried to dart away, but the Count was too quick for her. He grabbed her arm roughly and lowered his head, snarling in her ear.

'I am watching you. Very closely.'

'Is there a problem, Count?' Violet turned to see her father appear, looking concerned at the scene before him.

The Count put on a fake smile and started to stroke Violet's hair, making her shudder. 'None at all, I was just checking that my favourite little girl was having a lovely time. Now let us all go and have supper.'

Rose had saved Violet a seat next to her.

'Did the Count catch you?' she asked nervously.

'No, but I escaped through the window and he found me outside. He definitely suspects something,' Violet said. 'I can't believe the password is wrong. They must have changed it.'

She looked around for the pumpkin person, but they were nowhere to be seen.

The Count stood up and began making a long speech about how marvellous Isabella was, boasting on and on about her academic achievements and her sporting prowess. There was a polite round of applause and then the Count began on the Countess; her beauty, her fabulous taste and skill in renovating their house (with no mention of Violet's father, who smiled politely as he listened), how witty and clever she was. *Blah blah blah*, thought Violet. He finished by saying, 'So please, ladies and gentlemen, raise your glasses to Coraline, my one and only love, my Countess. You hold the key to my heart.' And he winked at his wife, who looked like the cat who'd got the cream.

'To Coraline!' everyone chorused politely, half-heartedly raising their glasses.

'That's it!' Violet whispered to Rose, who looked thoroughly confused. '"Key to my heart!" The safe was in the shape of a heart . . .

which means the password has to be Coraline.
I have to have one more go, for Dee Dee.'

Rose looked petrified at the idea of returning
upstairs. 'It's okay, I'll manage on my own,'
Violet said kindly. Rose was about to say that of
course she would help, but they were interrupted
by the Count making an announcement.

'Now you must all come outside to see the
stupendous firework display that Coraline
has created so cleverly.'

Perfect, thought Violet. Now all she had
to do was hang back from everyone and nip
back up the drainpipe. But the Count had
obviously had a word with Isabella, who
marched over to Violet.

'Violet, sweetie, come and watch the fireworks with me,' she said in the falsest voice imaginable, grabbing Violet's hand so she had no choice but to follow.

They stood right at the front of the crowd. Speakers had been set up and loud music began to boom out of them, as the sky was lit up with the multi-coloured plumes of rockets. Rose appeared by Violet's other side, giving her an idea of how she might escape from Isabella, who was still holding her hand in a crushing grip . . .

'*Aitchooo!*' Violet pretended to sneeze. '*Aitchoo!*' Isabella looked at her with distaste and allowed Violet to let go of her hand to blow her nose. Just then a mass of rockets went off, lighting up the sky.

While Isabella was distracted, Violet leaned over to Rose. 'Please, take her hand so she thinks it's me.'

Rose nodded in response and did as she had been asked. Isabella was so taken with the fireworks that she didn't notice Violet tiptoeing away.

Violet ran to the side of the house and shinned up the treacherous drainpipe. She was nearly at the top when it suddenly gave a dreadful lurch. Looking down, Violet saw the Count at the bottom of the drainpipe, his face a picture of rage. As the next round of fireworks lit up his deathly pale face, he took the drainpipe in both hands and pulled.

The drainpipe shook violently before entirely coming away from the wall. Violet gasped, preparing herself for a terrible fall, when something unexpected happened . . . .

A hand shot out of the open bedroom window, grabbed her and hauled her into the room.

All Violet saw was a flash of pumpkin suit as the person who had helped her ran out the door, whispering, 'Be quick! Very very quick!'

Violet dived to the back of the wardrobe. She punched C-O-R-A-L-I-N-E into the keypad. The door of the safe swung open, revealing Dee Dee's brooch sitting right in the middle of it, on a purple velvet cushion. With shaking hands Violet shoved the brooch into her pocket and scrambled back out of the cupboard.

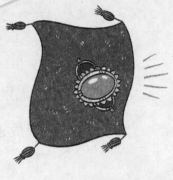

THE PARTY: PART 3 - TRICK OR TREAT?

But she was too late.

'What precisely do you think you're doing?' The Count was standing over her. He bent down so his face was right next to hers.

'Um . . .' Violet hesitated for a moment, horribly mesmerised by his face so close to hers.

'I think you had better give me back my brooch, don't you?' he said, menacingly.

Images span through Violet's head like a film: Dee Dee weeping, surrounded by packing cases; the Count and Countess toasting each other, before diving into an enormous swimming pool together. And suddenly Violet was no longer scared of the middle-aged man, covered

in melting makeup, who stood before her. No, she was furious with him.

'It's not yours, it's Dee Dee's and I'm getting it back for her. I know what you did. You got Dee Dee out of the way by giving her a theatre ticket, then you got Isabella to steal the Pearl. Then Mr Orger made a copy which you gave back to Dee Dee instead of the real jewel!'

The Count looked panicked for a moment, but he quickly pulled himself together. 'That's quite an accusation, Violet. I suppose you can prove it?' he sneered.

'Why else would you have been talking to Mr Orger the day after the Pearl was stolen?

Why else would you and your horrible wife have been toasting him the other night? And most importantly, why would you have Dee Dee's brooch in your safe?'

'How do you know it's not my brooch?' the Count asked. 'How do you know I did not see Dee Dee's jewel and love it so much that I had it copied, from memory, by my friend Mr Orger, as a present for my wife? Because that's my story and I'm sticking to it! So be a good little girl and give me back my brooch and we'll say no more about it.'

Violet had no intention of doing any such thing. And the time for words was over. She made a run for it.

'Not so fast!' the Count cried, lunging at her and grabbing her by the ear.

'Owww!' Violet shrieked, giving him a good kick in the shins.

'You little beast!' he roared. 'Now give it back or I'll really hurt you!' And he twisted her ear so the pain was excruciating.

At that precise moment the bedroom door opened and Rose ran in, accompanied by PC Green and another

couple of men, all looking extremely solemn.

The Count let go of Violet very quickly, but not quite quickly enough.

'Count, what on earth were you doing to Violet?' PC Green asked him, looking alarmed.

'Um, well,' began the Count, floundering around. 'We were just . . . er . . . playing a game, weren't we Violet?'

'No, not really,' Violet replied.

The Count swallowed hard. 'Rose, sweetie, I cannot believe you involved the police in such a matter. Inspector Green, I can explain everything—'

But the policeman interrupted him. 'It's back to PC Green and Rose didn't call me, she just showed me where you were. These gentlemen are from Scotland Yard's Incredibly Serious Crime Squad. There is a most suspiciously irregular issue with some business dealings of yours, apparently.'

One of the other gentlemen stepped forward. 'Count Du Plicitous, I am arresting you on the extremely strong suspicion of serious fraud and money laundering. You do not have to say anything – and in fact I would suggest you don't – but phone your lawyer immediately and get him to meet us at the station. Cuff him up, PC.'

The Count turned even paler and rivulets of sweat and makeup began to slide down his face.

Violet saw her chance and she jumped in.

'PC Green, you might also want to ask the Count exactly what he is doing with the Pearl of the Orient in his safe?'

The policeman raised his eyebrows questioningly at the Count. The Count smiled ingratiatingly back at him. 'As I was explaining to you, dear Violet, it is not the real Pearl of the Orient, but a copy I had made for my darling wife.'

'I think we both know that's a lie,' Violet said.

'Well prove it then!' the Count bellowed.

'Count! Really!' reprimanded PC Green. 'Shouting at a little girl! Now, Violet we have heard these accusations before. Do you have any proof this time?'

Violet thought for a moment. She didn't really have any proof at all . . .

'If you fetch Violet's mother she will be able to tell you if the brooch from the Count's safe is the real one or not,' Rose said, 'and if it is, we will all know he is lying.'

Violet grinned at her friend.

PC Green sent Rose off to find Camille and Benedict. They returned a few moments later.

'Violet!' they cried in unison. 'We have been looking for you everywhere! What is going on?'

'Plenty of time for explanations later,' PC

Green said, a little sternly. 'Now, madam, could you please tell us if this is the real Pearl of the Orient or a fake?'

Camille took the brooch in her hand and held it up to the light, turning it slowly this way and that. After a minute or two, she took a deep breath. 'It is real,' she announced. 'It is the Pearl of the Orient. One of the most valuable pieces of jewellery in the world.'

Everyone gasped, except the Count, who began to babble. 'Gentlemen, I can explain everything.

Please come and have a drink. I have some very fine triple malt whisky, or perhaps you prefer apricot brandy? Or peach schnapps? Please, I am sure we can sort this out.'

The men from Scotland Yard were having none of it.

'Cuff him, Green! This minute!'

The Countess and Isabella appeared just at that moment. An intense period of shrieking began as the Count was led away to the waiting police car.

PC Green turned to Violet. 'You were right all along, Violet, I'm sorry that I didn't believe you. Most impressive. Perhaps you should be adding amateur detective to your many other skills,' as the Count suggested?

'I couldn't have done it without Rose's help. She was really brave,' Violet told him.

'Good teamwork, girls.' The policeman nodded approvingly. 'Now I need to take this brooch back to Mrs Derota.'

'Oh, please can we take it?' Rose asked.

'I think that would be okay, just this once,' he replied with a smile, then wished them all a good night.

The girls searched for the pumpkin person to thank them for their help, but they had vanished.

The Countess was busy wailing in a corner with Isabella, and it seemed the wrong time to thank her for a lovely party, so instead Violet and Rose made their way out of the house and went to knock on Dee Dee's door.

'Happy Halloween!' they chorused when she opened the door.

'Aren't you supposed to say "trick or treat"?' Dee Dee said. 'Though I have to admit I'm

all out of sweets, my doorbell has been ring-a-ding-dinging all night. I'll have to take a trick. Do your worst!'

'Okay,' Violet said. 'Close your eyes and put out your hand.' And Violet placed the Pearl of the Orient on her outstretched palm.

Much later that night, when the moon had worked its way across the clear autumn sky, two couples met in the garden.

The first was Pudding and Lullabelle who sat happily together on the lawn.

And the second couple was Norma and Ernest, who were having a brief, whispered conversation. Ernest was dressed in his normal clothes and he had nearly managed to get all the orange makeup off his face and hands. They stood in the shadows and congratulated themselves that everything had worked out so well. For Dee Dee Derota, they both agreed, was a very nice lady.

After

About a week or so later, if you had happened to be standing outside one of the very smartest jewellers in Bond Street, you would have seen two ladies get out of a taxi and be ushered into the shop and to a small room upstairs.

Dee Dee and Camille were paying a visit to one of the most expert jewellers in the world, Señor Los Dideron.

There was a long silence while the Señor examined the jewel thoroughly. And then he came and knelt down in front of Dee Dee.

'Thank you Madame, for showing me the

most wonderful piece of jewellery I have ever had the pleasure of seeing in all my life.' He said in his thick Spanish accent. 'If I die tonight, I will die a happy man.'

Dee Dee let out a long and loud whoop of delight.

When the brooch was auctioned a few months later, a secret bidder paid such an enormous sum of money for it that the story made front page news around the world. Dee Dee would never have to worry about money again.

And the Count? Well, there's a rumour that he escaped from the police station by crawling out of a toilet window and was last seen scurrying onto his private jet with Coraline and Isabella in tow. But I couldn't possibly comment.

The Du Plicitous house stands empty except for Ernest who remains there, taking care of Chiang-Mai. He also spends a good deal of time helping his friend and neighbour, Dee Dee Derota, and drinking tea with his other good friend and neighbour, Norma.

And Violet? Both she and Rose were presented with very shiny medals by the Most Important Chief Inspector of All

Policemen and Mrs Rumperbottom dedicated an entire assembly at school to praising their ingenuity and bravery. Although really, Dee Dee being able to stay in her little flat was the only reward the girls wanted.

But now all the excitement has died down, I think Violet is nearly ready for another adventure . . .

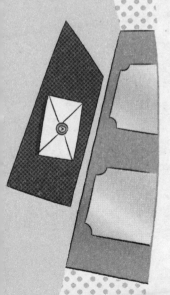

Violet's extra-helpful word glossary

Violet loves words, especially if they sound unusual, so some of the words used in her story might have been a little tricky to understand. Most of them you probably know, but Violet has picked out a few to explain...

Architect — My father is an architect and it keeps him very busy! He designs houses and buildings for other people.

Chérie — My mother is from France and I love it when she speaks to me in French! Chérie means darling, angel, sweetie, cutie-pie, honey or anything else like that.

Enchanté — This is a very fancy (and French) way of saying 'pleased to meet you'.

Merci — I'm sure you know this word? Yes, that's right, it means thank you in French, so it's an important one to remember!

N'est-ce pas — Godmother Celeste said this

to my mother when she was teasing her about being naughty. It means 'isn't it?' in French

Duplicitous — After the Count had been arrested, my father told me that duplicitous means someone who is sneaky and dishonest... so their name should really have given away the family were crooks!

Pedigree — Chiang Mai is a pedigree Siamese cat as the Du Plicitous family liked to tell people! It means an animal who has a family tree of very grand relatives.

Eccentric — This is how I think of Dee Dee instead of 'odd' or 'weird'. It's someone who is unusual, but, I think, in a lovable way.

Costume Jewellery — the Du Plicitouses swtched the Pearl of the Orient for a fake jewel. This kind of jewellery can be called costume jewellery, it can be just as beautiful and look just like the real thing. Sometimes only an expert, can tell it apart from real jewellery.

Starlet – This is what Dee Dee was. It means a young and famous actress.

Southern Belle – Dee Dee had to explain this to me. A Southern Belle is a stylish lady who lives in the southern states of America and has a very particular accent. They say things like 'well, I do declare' and 'Fiddle de dee!'.

Marilyn Monroe – Marilyn was a very famous actress. Dee Dee told me that she even once sang Happy Birthday to the President!

Frank Sinatra – I bet if you ask any grown-up they'll have heard of this actor and singer. Dee Dee says he wanted to marry her, but she fell in love with Dave Derota instead.

Kerfuffle – I love this word! It means a commotion, noise or rumpus. I think it's really fun to say.

Alibi – Isabella had a fake one of these . . . it's an explanation of where someone is at the time of a crime.

Fjords — Celeste visited these in Norway and said they were very beautiful. They are a narrow strip of sea in-between cliffs, I'm hoping next time she goes she'll take me!

The Pearl of the Orient — The Jewel has had a very dramatic past! My mother told me it was found a long time ago by pearl divers in South China and then the Persian Emperor paid lots of money to buy it. His great, great, great, great grandson gave it to his favourite girlfriend who took it and ran off with one of his footmen! She sold it to a very American lady who only wore it once before it was stolen by the famous jewel thief, the Leopard. Everyone thought it was gone forever until Dee Dee revealed it in her biscuit tin!

Have you solved all the Violet mysteries?